Say hello to the Bunnykins!

Father Mother

William

Susan

Tom

Polly

Harry

Baby

Written by Nicola Baxter
Illustrated by Frank Endersby

Manufactured under licence by
Bookmart Limited, Desford Road, Enderby, Leicester LE9 5AD

Published by Bookmart Limited
Registered Number 2372865
Trading as Bookmart Limited
Desford Road Enderby Leicester LE9 5AD

ISBN 1-85605-915-4

Produced for Bookmart Limited by Nicola Baxter
PO Box 71 Diss Norfolk IP22 2DT

Designed by Amanda Hawkes

Printed in Singapore

Bunnykins

By
Royal Doulton

Susan's Could-Be-Carrot Cake

AND

Father's Super System

Susan's
Could-Be-Carrot Cake

One day Mother Bunnykins woke to find that her nose was sniffly and her ears were wiffly. If you are a bunny, you'll understand exactly how that feels. Father Bunnykins insisted she must stay in bed all day. "We'll do everything," he said.

Downstairs, the little bunnies were already having their breakfast. When their father told them about poor Mother Bunnykins' cold, they felt very sorry for her.

"I'll make a Get-Better-Soon card," said Tom. And Harry ran to get *his* paints, too. Polly decided to do some dusting, while William went out to help his father in the garden. Only Susan wasn't sure how to help.

7

The other little bunnies had kindly left the table without thinking about the washing up, so Susan piled up the plates and bowls and carried them to the kitchen sink. The kitchen always reminded Susan of Mother Bunnykins. It was warm and friendly, just like her. As Susan looked around, she started to think about what Mother Bunnykins would do if one of her little ones was feeling poorly.

Suddenly, Susan knew what she could do to help. Mother Bunnykins always made her special carrot cake whenever anyone was ill. Susan could make one too!

Susan whizzed around the kitchen. She finished the washing up in no time. Then she put on her mother's large apron and began to weigh out ingredients.

Soon she was beating butter and sugar into a creamy mixture and adding eggs and some walnuts from the cupboard. Now for the carrots. Susan looked in the vegetable basket. There were no carrots! Perhaps some new ones needed to be dug up. She took off her apron and trotted out into the garden.

But Father Bunnykins shook his head. "There'll be no more carrots until the new crop is ready in a few weeks' time," he said. "But I can give you some lovely parsnips."

Susan thought about it for a moment. Parsnips were *almost* like carrots, weren't they?

That afternoon, when Susan's cake was cooked and cooled and iced, the little bunnies trooped upstairs to see how Mother Bunnykins was feeling. Susan came last of all, carrying a tray with a pot of tansy tea and her beautiful cake.

Luckily, Mother Bunnykins was feeling *much* better. When she had admired Tom's and Harry's cards, cuddled Polly and congratulated William on his weeding, she looked at Susan's tray.

"I'm ready for a slice of your delicious cake now, Susan," she said. "How clever you were to make it!" Susan watched anxiously as her mother took her first nibble. And then another. And another!

"It's *wonderful!*" cried Mother Bunnykins. "I feel completely well again! But how did you manage? There weren't any carrots left, were there?"

"Actually, it's not carrot cake," said Susan slowly. "It's … er … it's could-be-carrot cake."

"All cooks have their secrets," smiled Mother Bunnykins, "so I won't ask for yours. Could I have another slice, please? A big one!"

Father's
Super System

Father Bunnykins stood in the garden one day and shook his head gravely. "That fence at the back needs painting," he said.
"It's looking dreadfully shabby.
And while I'm about it,
it might be fun to change
the colour this time. Now,
what should it be?"

"Red!" cried William, "like my jacket! It's my favourite colour in all the world."

"No, it should be blue!" said Susan, "like my dress. Blue is a lovely colour." But the other little bunnies didn't agree. Tom and Harry wanted green. Polly liked pink best. And even the baby yelled "ewoo", which the others thought might mean yellow.

So Father Bunnykins did what he
always did on these occasions – he
went off to ask Mother. As seven
eager faces looked at her, Mother
Bunnykins didn't know what to
say. She couldn't bear to
disappoint any of them.

Just in time, she had a brilliant idea. "Why not use
all the colours?" she suggested. "It could be a striped
fence! There wouldn't be another one like it in all of
Little Twitching. And you can each help to do the
painting. Only please, my dears, do, do remember
that paint won't wash off your clothes. And don't let
Baby fall in a paint pot!"

Pretty soon, each one of the little Bunnykins had a paintbrush, a stirring stick and a pot of paint, although Father thought it might be better if Baby's pot was left closed for the time being. She could just pretend.

"Now then, painters!" called Father. "Stand by your paint pots! Now, take up your stirring sticks and … wait for it, wait for it … that means you, too, William … *stir!* One, two, three! Right down to the bottom, Polly! Now dip in your brushes. Just a little bit, Harry! Ready? Watch out for drips and … two steps forward … mind Mother's dahlias, Tom, and … up, down, up, down!"

The bunnies stood back with pride to admire their pretty painted panels. But Father didn't let them rest.

"Finished one panel? Now, six steps to the left. That's *this* way, Polly! Dip in your brushes! *Much* better, Harry! Don't drip on Baby! Everybody ready? Two steps forward … wait until I give the word, Tom, *and* … up, down, up, down! That's wonderful!"

It was enormous fun painting the fence, but Father Bunnykins' excellent system didn't work well for very long.

For a start, the older bunnies painted much more quickly than the younger ones. Then Tom leaned over and got paint on his ears. William got so carried away that he painted over a panel Father had already done, leaving a swirly-whirly mess. And Baby got tired of pretending and went to sleep.

"All right! That's enough!" cried Father, feeling his ears going floppy with frustration. "Come with me, everyone, and I'll show you how to clean your brushes. And your ears, too, Tom!"

"Can we do some more painting tomorrow?" asked Harry, as they all sat down to supper. Mother and Father Bunnykins exchanged glances.

"Yes, you can," said Mother. "You can all paint me a beautiful picture to put on the kitchen wall. That's the kind of painting I like to see."

19

When the little ones were all in bed that evening, Mother and Father Bunnykins went out into the garden and looked at the fence for a long time. Then they laughed until tears dripped off the ends of their whiskers.

I'll ask Uncle Sammy to come and give me a hand with it tomorrow," said Father at last. "I've always thought white was a good colour for a fence!"

"I couldn't agree more," chuckled Mother Bunnykins. "I don't know whose idea *this* was!"

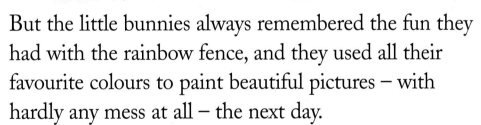

But the little bunnies always remembered the fun they had with the rainbow fence, and they used all their favourite colours to paint beautiful pictures – with hardly any mess at all – the next day.